We dedicate this book to all the daring young adventurers out there. Every journey is BETTER TOGETHER, and we're with you every step of the way.
—Drew and Jonathan Scott

ISBN 978-0-06-284665-5

by Drew and Jonathan Scott
The artist used Adobe Photoshop to create the illustrations for this book.
Typography by Rick Farley
19 20 21 22 23 PC 10 9 8 7 6 5 4 3 2 1

❖

First Edition

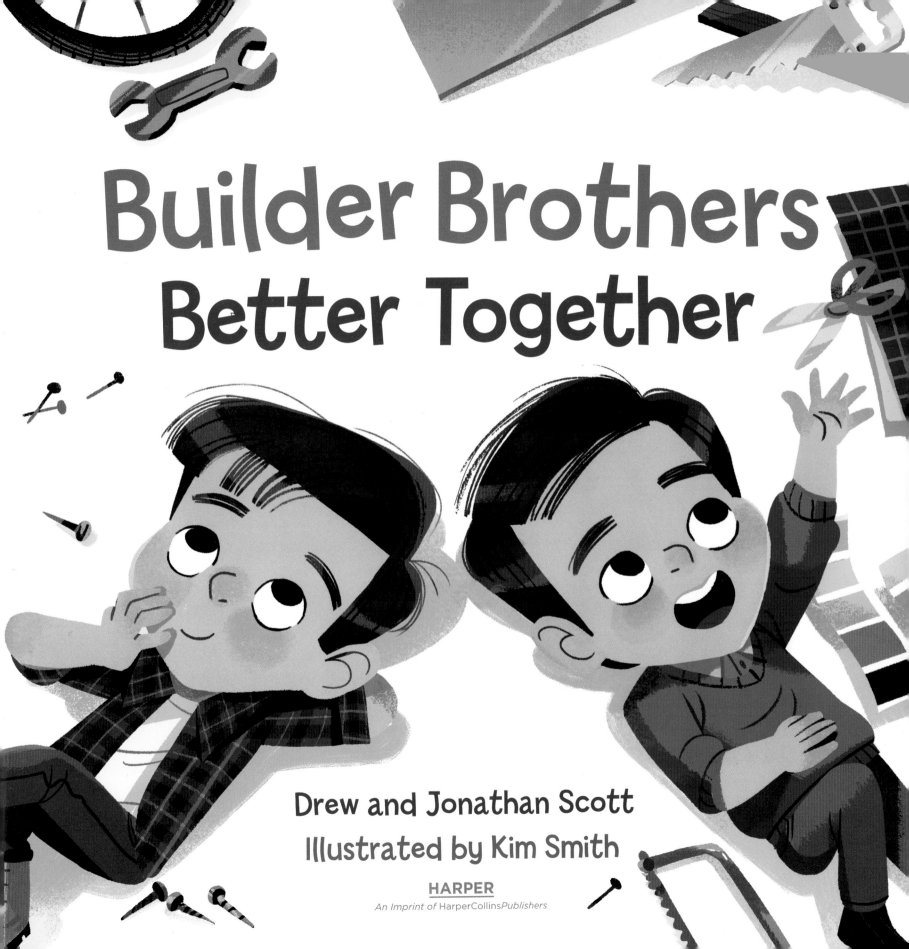

Builder Brothers
Better Together

Drew and Jonathan Scott

Illustrated by Kim Smith

HARPER

An Imprint of HarperCollinsPublishers

Drew and Jonathan are identical twins, and they're also each other's best friend. They go everywhere together and they do everything together. Until one day . . .

"Look!" cried Jonathan. "There, in the window!"
Their town was sponsoring a Soap Box Derby race.

"It says we get to build our own race car," said Drew.
"And they've got prizes too," said Jonathan.

"Oh yeah—we're in it to win it!" the brothers cried.

"To the hardware store!"

"We should build the lightest car," said Drew. "Lighter means a fast start."

"We should build the heaviest car," said Jonathan. "Heavier means more momentum downhill."

"Streamlined is better," said Drew.

"Bigger is better," said Jonathan.

The more they talked, the less they agreed.

When the brothers got home, they were *still* arguing.

"He hates all my ideas," Jonathan complained.

"No, he hates mine," Drew shot back.

Mom shook her head. "Remember, boys, teamwork makes the dream work. It's always better when you work together."

But the brothers wouldn't listen.

"I'm building my own racer," said Jonathan.

"Me too," said Drew. . . .

They each designed—

Scribble, scribble, scrabble

—and sawed—

VOOMPA, VOOMPA, SHOOMPA

—and hammered—

bim, bim, BAM!

—their own cars.

"I'm taking home that prize tomorrow," said Drew.
"Not if I take it first," said Jonathan.

On race day, the brothers pushed their cars into the waiting zone. Jonathan and Drew shook hands. "May the best man win!" they said. "Or woman," Rapid Rita, last year's winner, corrected them. "Right—may the best person win," they agreed, but all the while, each was thinking, *That's me!*

Everyone lined up for the race down Hawkeye Hill.

KA-*POW!* went the starting gun.

And away they rolled!

WHOOSH!

Rounding the first curve, Jonathan pulled ahead of the pack. Try as he might, Drew's car hung near the rear. *Maybe Jonathan was right*, he thought. *Heavier is better.*

But when he rounded the second curve, he saw . . .

Jonathan's car had broken an axle. It was *too* heavy.
He was out of the race!

Drew bit his lip. He knew Jonathan's car wouldn't have gotten so heavy if they hadn't been trying so hard to one-up each other. He had only a split second to make a decision, but he knew there was only one decision to make.

"I'm missing my copilot," said Drew as he pulled over. "Need a lift?"

"Teamwork makes the dream work!!" cried Jonathan. "I'm in!"

They quickly added Jonathan's spoiler to the back of Drew's car,

gave a push, and hopped inside.

With both boys on board, the car was heavier!
It zipped past the Corncob—

and the Shark—

and the Ratmobile—

As the finish line approached, they were just a hair behind the leader, Rapid Rita. . . .

And that's exactly where they finished.
Second place! *So close!*
The twins congratulated Rita and took their second-place prize.

"I think we learned something," said Jonathan.

"Yeah," said Drew. "Even though we had different ideas, they were both good ideas."

"Next time, let's team up sooner!"
"You got it," said Drew. "There's nothing we can't do as a team, because we're always . . ."

"Better together!" they cried.

Build your own mini race car!

You can build your own mini race car using stuff from around the house.

Important: Do not do this activity without adult supervision.

Here's what you need:

- ☐ One cardboard toilet paper roll (empty)
- ☐ Bright paints
- ☐ Paintbrush
- ☐ Sheet of cardboard
- ☐ Pencil
- ☐ Marker
- ☐ Scissors or craft knife
- ☐ Glue
- ☐ Small, pronged brads
- ☐ Figurine (optional)

Instructions:

Step 1. Clean all the toilet paper off the roll.

Step 2. Paint the roll to look like a race car.

Step 3. Draw four big circles on the cardboard for the car's tires, and one smaller one for the steering wheel.

Step 4. Cut out circles and paint them appropriately.

Step 5. After all the paint has dried, ask an adult to cut a U-shaped opening in the toilet paper roll then fold it back to look like a seat.

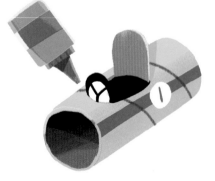

Step 6. Glue the painted steering wheel on the opposite side of the opening from the seat.

Step 7. Poke the brads through the wheels and car body, opening the prongs to hold them in place.

Step 8. Add a toy driver (if you have one), and you're ready to race!